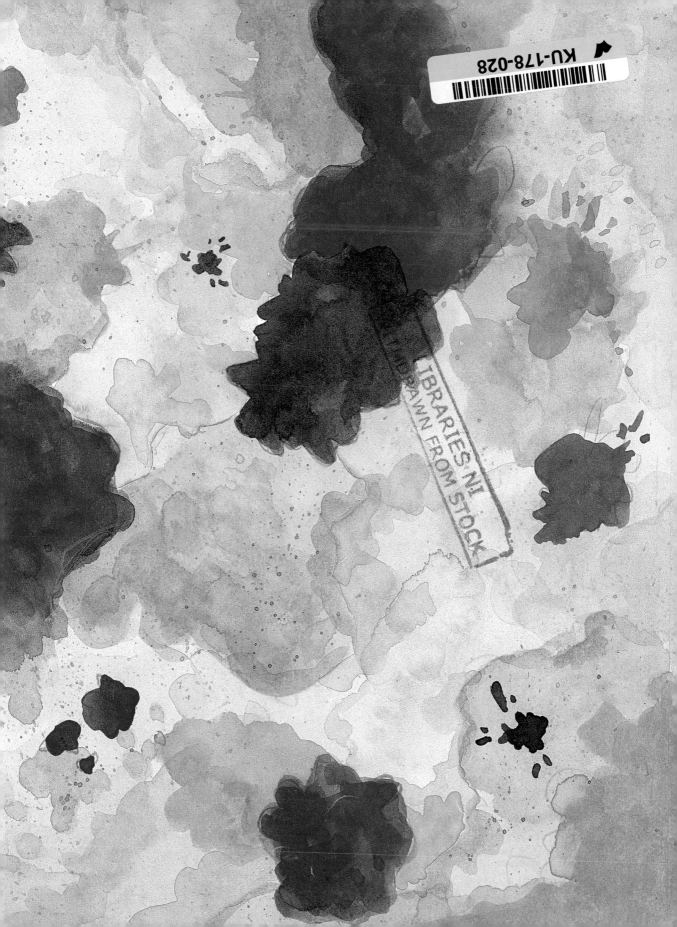

A TEMPLAR BOOK

First published in the UK in 2017 by Templar Publishing,
an imprint of Kings Road Publishing,
part of the Bonnier Publishing Group,
The Plaza, 535 King's Road, London, SW10 0SZ
www.bonnierpublishing.com

1 3 5 7 9 10 8 6 4 2

ISBN 978-1-78370-830-7 (Hardback)
ISBN 978-1-78741-093-0 (Paperback)

Designed by Kieran Hood
Edited by Ruth Symons

Printed in China

Crocodali

Lucy Volpin

templar publishing

Do you mind? I'm very busy here.

I am Crocodali, the most talented painter in the whole wide world. And **you** are in **my** studio!

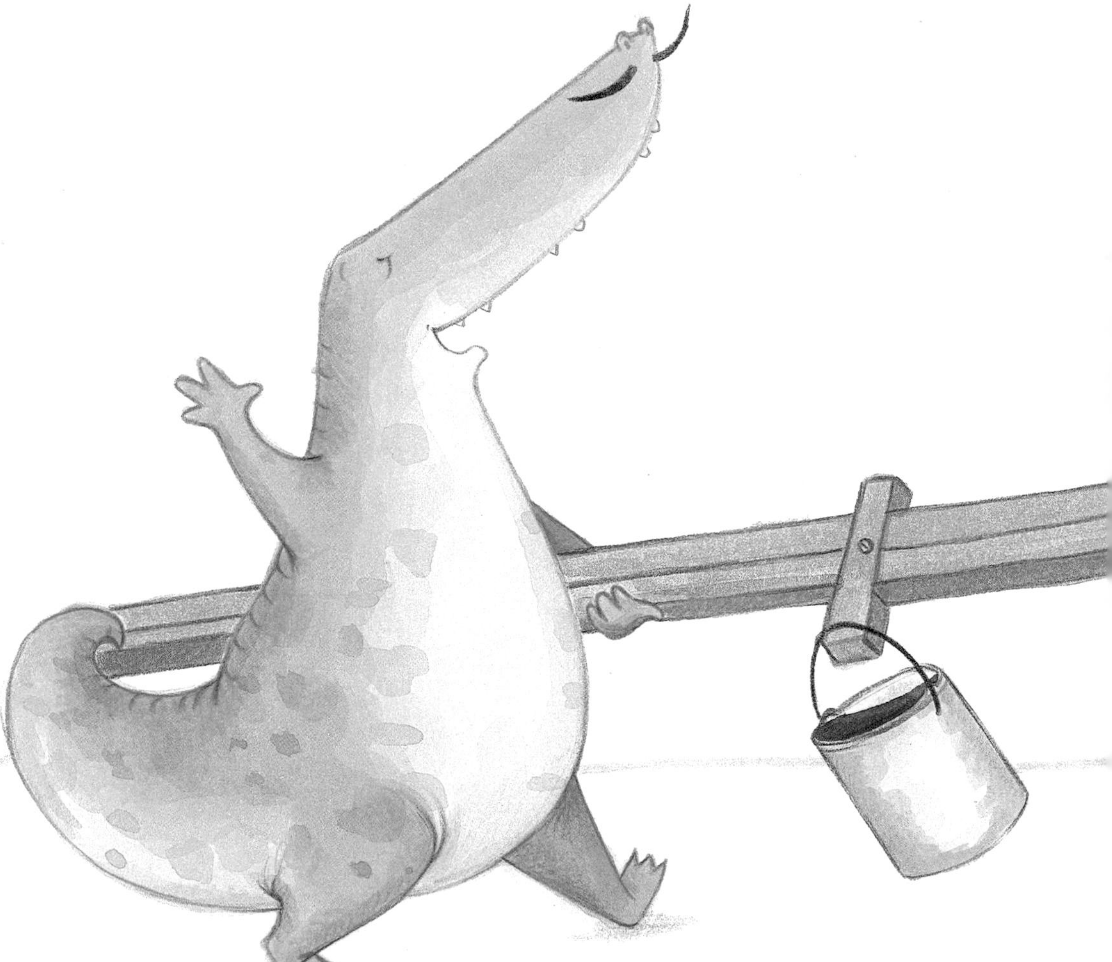

I'm sorry, I have no time for signings today.
I am about to create a masterpiece . . .

The thing is, I just can't quite get this canvas straight. Now that you're here, you might as well help.

Could you tilt the book to the right?

That should do it.

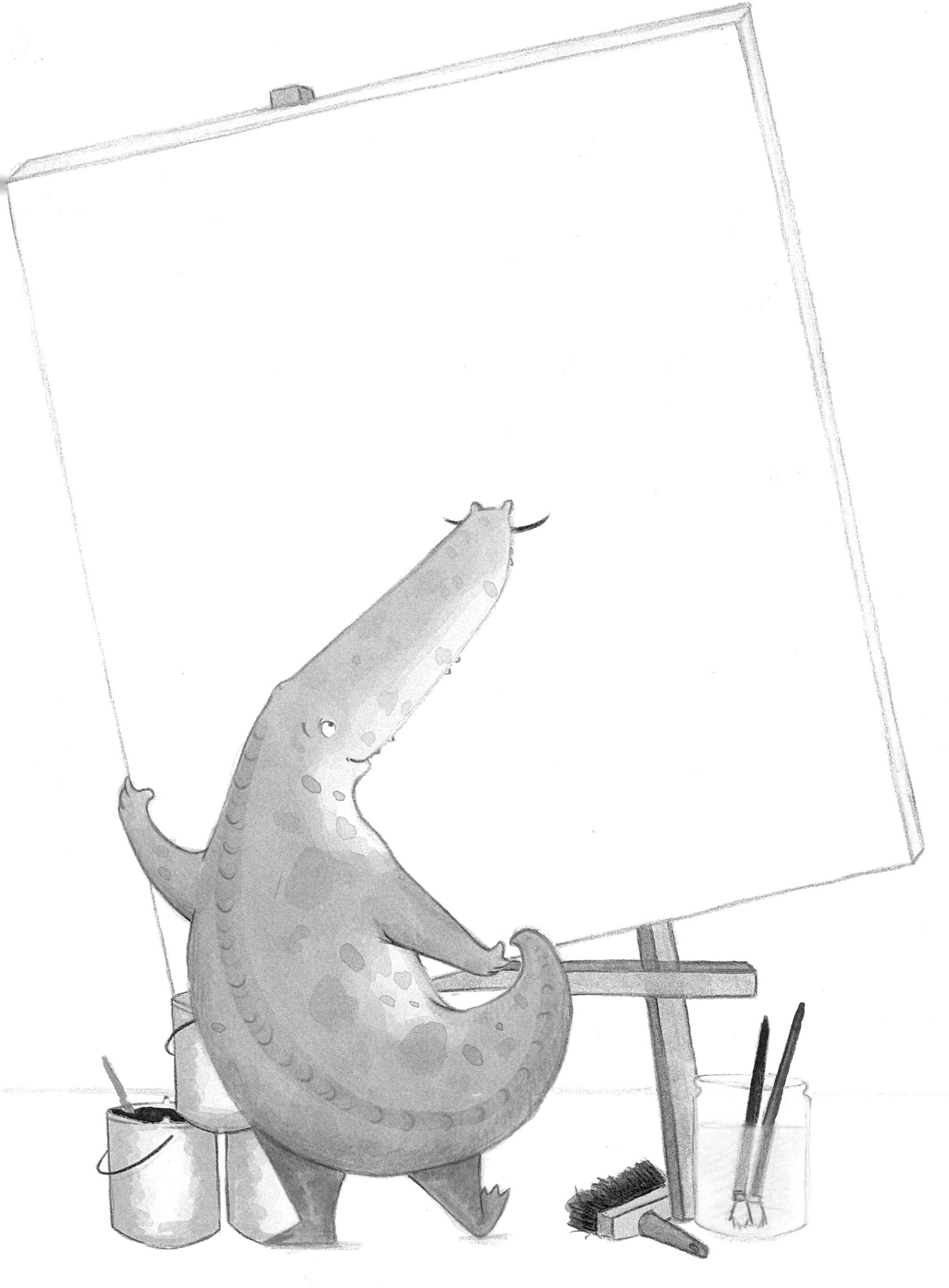

Oh no, you've tilted it **much** too far.
What am I going to do?

You'll have to tilt it to the left now.
Go on.

Just a little this time.

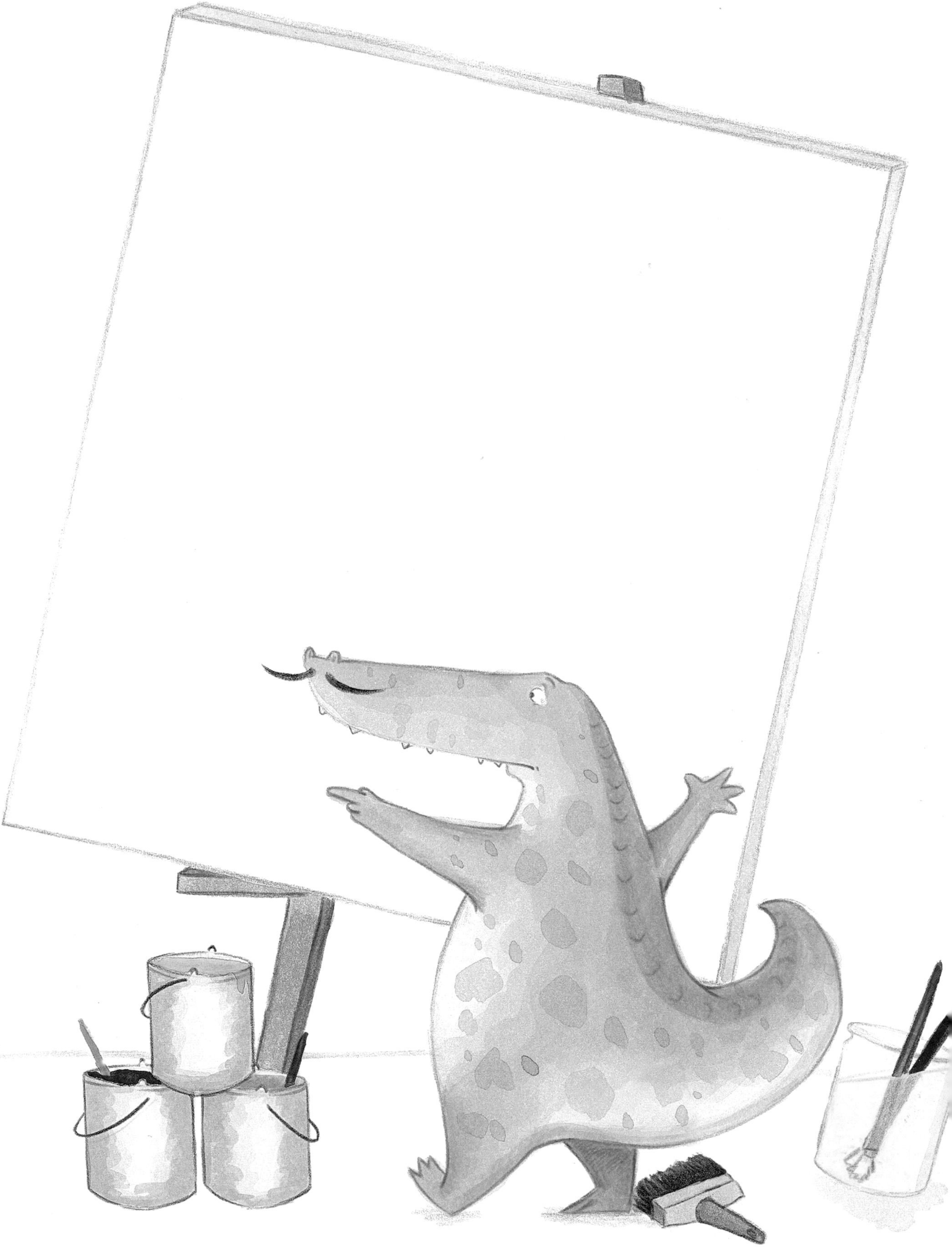

I said 'just a little'. . .

This is a disaster.
My paints have gone everywhere!

You've done enough for today.
Just sit there and read while I clean up.
And don't you dare move a thing!

Did you turn the page?
I knew I shouldn't have trusted you.
I'll have to start all over again.

But hang on . . . that looks quite nice.
Maybe you're not so useless after all.

Give the book a shake and see what happens.

NOT

SO
HARD!

Now the paint's all over me too! I'll never get clean. I hope you're feeling pleased with yourself.

Let's get this place tidied up.

But wait, look at that. I think I like it!
Though is it upside down?

I'll just turn it around and
add some finishing touches . . .

A dab of purple . . .

. . . some yellow, some red . . .

. . . and then a good mix.

Are you helping or not?
Go on – rub the canvas.

It's a masterpiece! I really **am** the greatest painter in the world.

Now I'll put it over here to dry.
But maybe we could speed things up a bit.
Could you blow on the painting?

Three, two, one . . .

BLOW!

Oh . . .

Let’s start again!

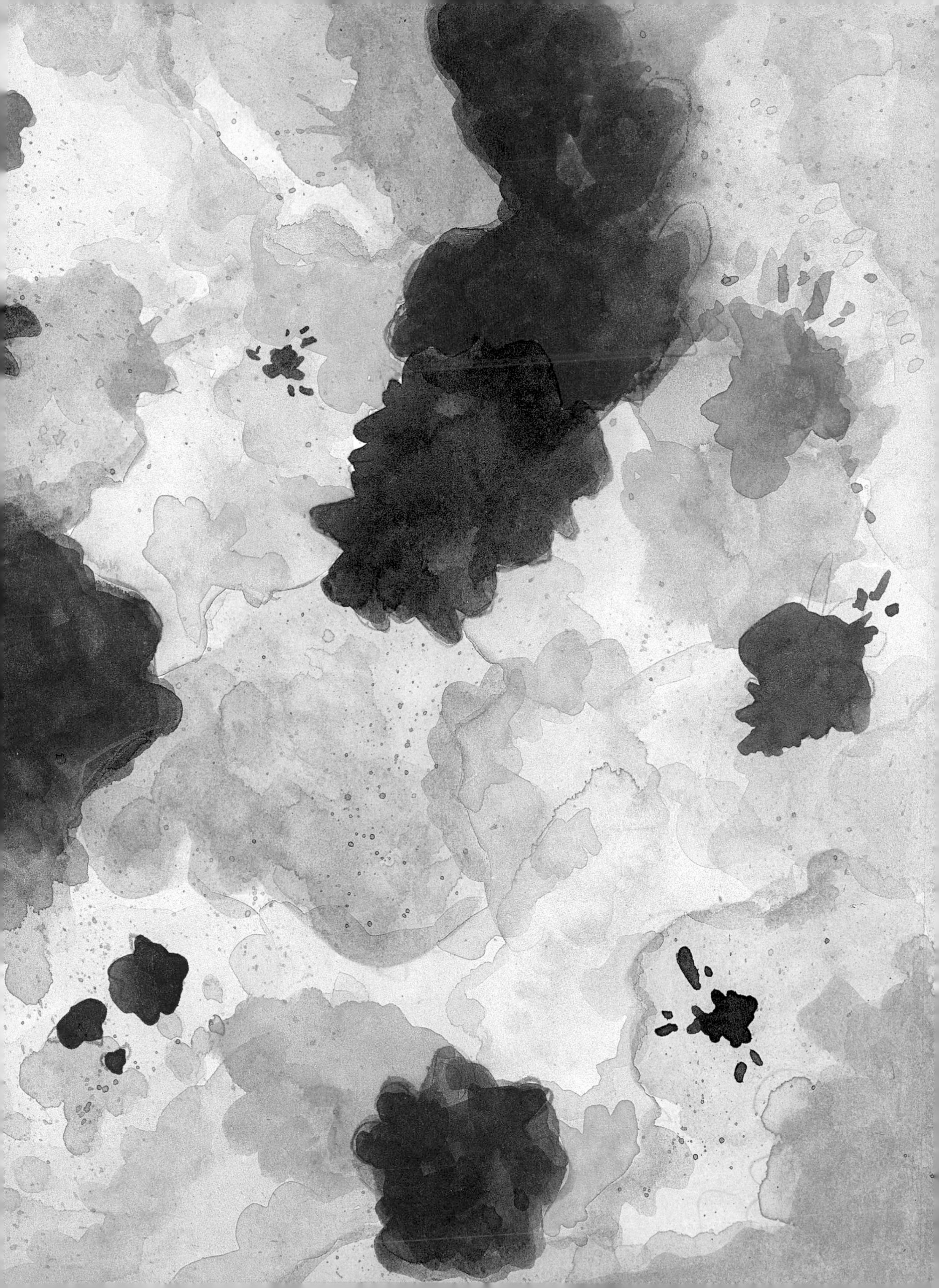

More picture books from Templar:

ISBN: 978-1-78370-667-9 (Hardback)

ISBN: 978-1-78370-653-2 (Hardback)
978-1-78370-795-9 (Paperback)

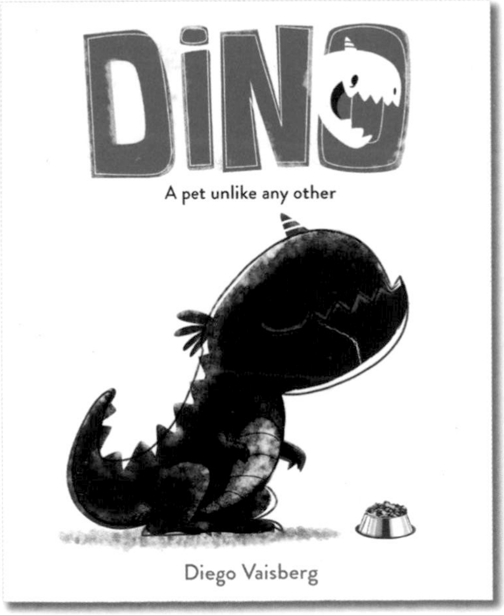

ISBN: 978-1-78370-671-6 (Hardback)

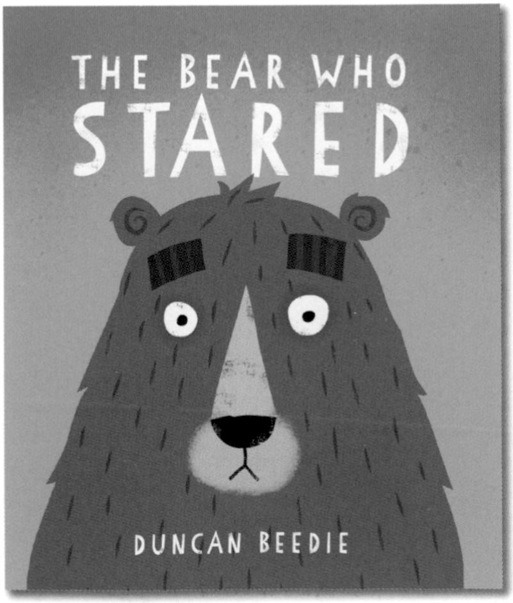

ISBN: 978-1-78370-374-6 (Hardback)
978-1-78370-375-3 (Paperback)